Alphonse
and the
Stonehenge
Mystery

JIM SMITH

First published in Great Britain by World's Work Ltd, 1979
Fircone Books edition 2011
Text and illustrations copyright © Jim Smith 1979
ISBN 978-1-907700-03-3

Visit our website at www.firconebooks.com
Design by Dot Little. Printed and bound in China.

MIX
Paper from
responsible sources
FSC® C008047

Fircone Books

Alphonse le Flic, eminent detective, and Mole McGrath, ace reporter, had been asked by Scotland Yard to investigate the rumours of strange lights and night-time noises at Stonehenge.

A group of people had gathered round one of the stones. "What is it?" Alphonse asked.

"That young pig, there," he was told, "he was sharpening his penknife on the stone when it collapsed!" Alphonse looked at the heap on the ground. "A rubber inflatable imitation!" he shouted.

Mole and Alphonse decided to keep watch that night on Stonehenge. At the darkest hour, when they were dropping into an uneasy sleep, a car drew up. Out stepped a figure.

The figure flashed a torch, and Mole immediately recognised him. "It's Nick Gristle!" he whispered, "Scotland Yard have been after him for years!"

A droning noise in the sky made them look up. The noise came nearer and nearer until it stopped overhead. Nick Gristle flashed his torch upwards, and in answer a bright beam of light shone down on to a stone.

A metal grab followed the light, and Nick Gristle climbed up a ladder to fix the hook to the massive stone. He signalled to the sky again, and then jumped clear. Slowly, the stone was pulled out of the ground like a gigantic tooth!

The bright light was switched off, and the noise faded away as the stone disappeared into the night. Nick Gristle hurriedly put a replacement in the hole and pumped it up.

Dawn was breaking as Nick drove away. Mole and Alphonse waited for a minute, and then followed.

"We may be able to find out where the stones are being hidden!" Alphonse said hopefully.

They followed Nick Gristle's three-wheeled car until they reached Dimpsey, on the edge of a moor. Nick stopped at a café, and Mole and Alphonse went in after him, and ordered a late breakfast.

Nick seemed very agitated. "Perhaps he is waiting for someone," suggested Mole. Sure enough, he was soon joined by a companion. Alphonse gasped when he saw who it was, and hid behind his menu. "It's Wolfgang the Pink Baron!" he muttered, "my old wartime enemy!"

Alphonse listened in silence to their conversation, and learned that an American millionaire wanted the rarest rock garden in the world. One more stone was needed from Stonehenge to complete it.

Without warning, Wolfgang jumped up. "Come Nick! We have more work to do!" As they left the café and drove away in Nick's car, Mole and Alphonse followed at a distance.

"We must have taken a wrong turning!" Alphonse moaned, when he realised that he had lost the three-wheeled car. Mole looked around for wheel marks. "It's hopeless," he complained, leaning back on a milestone, "we'll never find them now. *Aargh!*"

Alphonse turned to see Mole disappear as the milestone gave way.
"Look Mole!" he cried as he climbed down. There was the
three-wheeler, which had been hidden in the entrance of a rocky
underground tunnel.

Silently, Mole and Alphonse crept down the passage until it opened onto a quarry. Hiding behind some packing cases, they peered out.

In front of them, tethered to the ground and filling the quarry, was the most enormous airship! And in the corner of the quarry were the missing pieces of Stonehenge. It was the perfect hiding place. "So that's how they did it!" said Alphonse. From the bustle, he realised that another trip was about to be made. He would have to act fast.

He whispered his plan to Mole, and they ran back down the passage, and drove at breakneck speed to a nearby private airfield belonging to an old friend of Alphonse. As Alphonse started the engine of a two-seater plane, Mole rang the local police station and his newspaper office.

With the sun beginning to set, Wolfgang the Pink Baron steered his clumsy airship out of the quarry, and headed towards Stonehenge for the last time.

He was happily cruising along when he saw a bi-plane bearing down on a collision course! At the very last minute, it turned sharply away.

"Whew!" Wolfgang breathed, but the plane returned, and flew close to the airship's control cabin. The pilot signalled Wolfgang to land, and then he recognised his old enemy, Alphonse.

"You don't frighten me!" Wolfgang shouted angrily, and he shook his fist as the plane flew off. Then, out of the setting sun, Alphonse suddenly appeared again, flying straight for the airship!

Wolfgang began to panic. He knew a collision would mean an instant explosion. "Abandon ship!" he ordered, as he opened the valves to release the inflammable gas from the balloon. The crew bailed out, and Wolfgang steered his airship down to make a crash landing.

Alphonse and Mole were delighted to see their plan working. They leaned out of the plane, laughing, and pointed to the parachutes and the sinking airship. Then to their horror, their engine coughed, spluttered and stopped. They realised the plane was in a steep dive!

Before Alphonse could re-start the engine, they crashed into the woods
outside Dimpsey. Leaving the plane balancing dangerously on the
tree-tops, Alphonse and Mole crawled out, and tumbled to the ground.

On the other side of town, Wolfgang's airship rested gently on the roof-tops, jammed between the chimneys. "Help!" Wolfgang cried, spotting Nick Gristle in the street far below.

Propping his ladder up against a lamppost, Nick climbed up to grab
Wolfgang as he swung down from the abandoned airship.

Wolfgang jumped into Nick's car just as Alphonse and Mole arrived.
"Ha ha!" he laughed as the three-wheeler sped past the breathless pair.
Alphonse was furious! "I'll catch you yet!" he shouted after him.

Mole was wondering what had happened to the police, when he heard a tremendous crash. "Come on Alphonse!" he yelled.

They headed into the woods, meeting the police on the way, and what a scene they found! Alphonse's plane had fallen from its landing place on the tree-tops, through the branches, and had finally crashed on to the front of the getaway three-wheeler.

Alphonse was overjoyed when the police locked up the shaken stone thieves. "At last!" he said. "I've captured the Pink Baron!"